Johnny Mutton,

He's So Him!

STORIES AND PICTURES
BY JAMES PROIMOS

HARCOURT, INC.

SAN DIEGO   NEW YORK   LONDON

www.HarcourtBooks.com

Library of Congress Cataloging-in-Publication Data
Proimos, James.
Johnny Mutton: he's so him!/stories and pictures by James Proimos.
p. cm.
Summary: A kindhearted sheep in human clothing enjoys entering
a cooking contest, planning a birthday party, and participating in a
staring contest, but each event has an unexpected result.
[1. Sheep—Fiction.   2. Humorous stories.]   I. Title.
PZ7.P9432Jq   2003
[E]—dc21   2002001573
ISBN 0-15-216760-9

First edition

A C E G H F D B

Manufactured in China

The illustrations in this book were first drawn with a pen,
then colorized in Adobe Photoshop.
The display type was set in Heatwave.
The text type was set in Tykewriter.
Color separations by Colourscan Co. Pte. Ltd., Singapore
Manufactured by South China Printing Company, Ltd., China
This book was printed on totally chlorine-free Enso Stora Matte paper.
Production supervision by Sandra Grebenar and Ginger Boyer
Designed by Barry Age

For Ro Stimo

The Stories

Johnny Mutton Saves the Universe

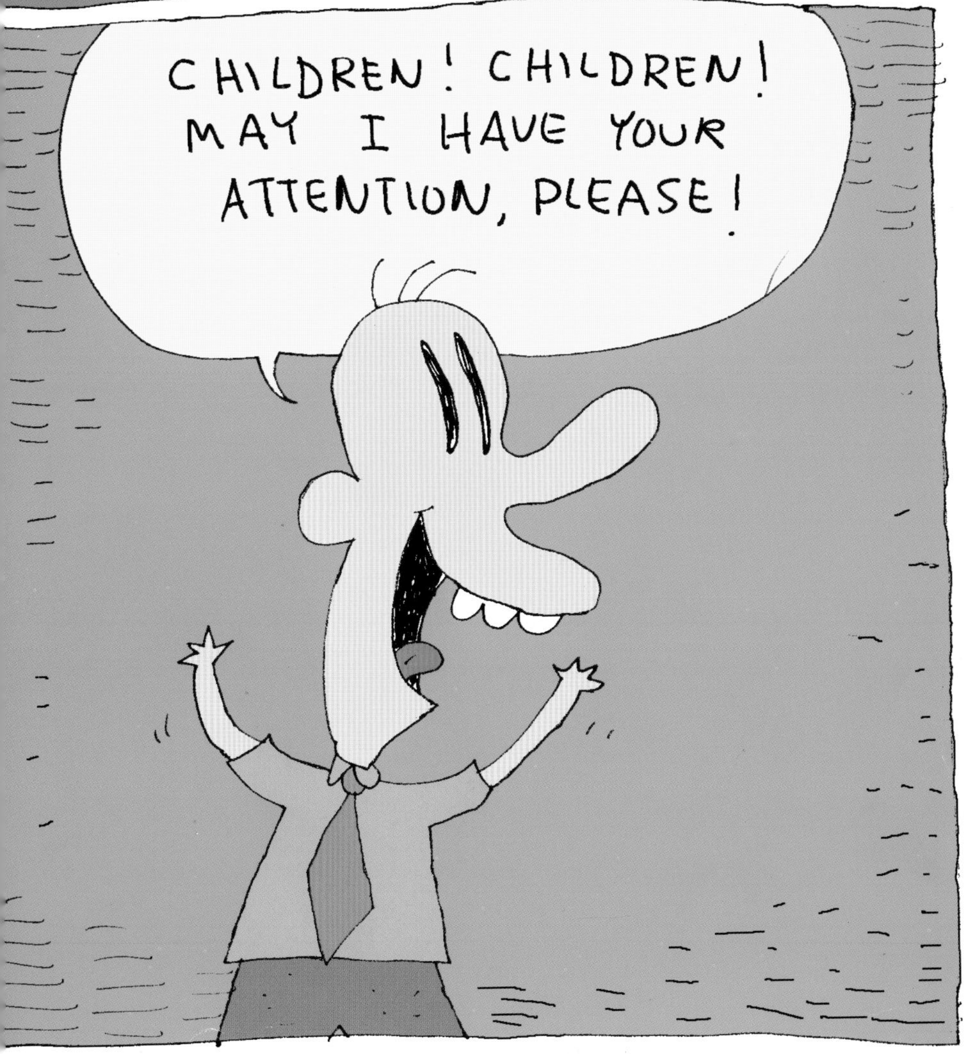

IT'S THAT WONDERFUL TIME OF YEAR AGAIN!
YAHOO
SCIENCE FAIR!
BOO

3

The Sweet Baby Doll 5000 was Johnny's idea of the perfect robot.

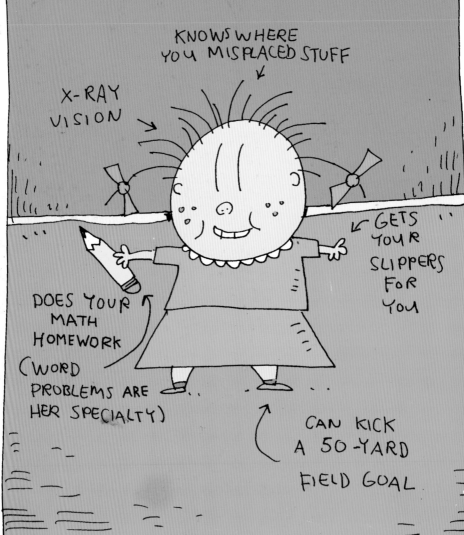

MOMMA, I NEED SUGAR, SPICE, A LIGHTBULB, NINE "D" BATTERIES, A RUBBER BAND, DUCT TAPE, AND A BOWL OF PASTA.

YOU NEED A BOWL OF PASTA TO BUILD THE SWEET BABY DOLL 5000?

NAH, I'M JUST KINDA HUNGRY.

Seven hours later.

LOOK, IT'S FINISHED! GET MOMMA HER SLIPPERS.

HOW CUTE!

CHOMP!

5

And that is how Johnny Mutton
saved the universe.

The Cook-Off

Mandy Dinkus was a fantastic cook.
Well, at least that's what she was
constantly telling people.

THAT IS TOTALLY WRONG!

27
+13
_____
I'M A
FANTASTIC
COOK !

I KNOW.

YET
IT IS
TRUE.

Then one day Dinkus went too far.

I AM THE BEST COOK IN THE WORLD!

HMM.

NOT BETTER THAN MY MOMMA, YOU'RE NOT!

HA! YOUR MOMMA ISN'T FIT TO WEAR MY OVEN MITTS!

GASP

EVEN I CAN OUTCOOK YOU!

I CHALLENGE YOU TO A COOK-OFF!

Johnny concocted an elaborate contract filled with rules, regulations, and cash prizes. Mandy and Johnny both signed it.

The rules and regulations for the COOK-OFF!

1. Cook something good.
2. Cook it by yourself.
3. Bring it to the park by 2 p.m. tomorrow.
4. Present it to the judges (the Winslow triplets).
5. Winner gets a kazoo, a yo-yo, all the change in my shoe box, and the thrill of victory.
6. Loser can't say, "I'm a fantastic cook!" for the rest of her livelong days.
7. Let the fun begin!

Johnny   Mandy

Johnny spent the morning of the contest
making the most magical food
he could think of....

CUPCAKES!

Johnny loaded his wagon with cupcakes and headed to the park. But along the way, he met a few folks in need of magic.

Mutton arrived at the park just in time to appear before the judges.

Lucky for Johnny, Mandy Dinkus made something so adult the smell alone turned the judges green.

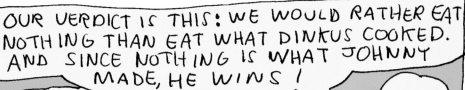

Johnny was happy about winning. But he was even happier about the new friends he had made that day.

Party Animal

It was one week before her birthday, and Gloria Crust was doing her best to get Johnny to plan a party for her.

BOY, IT SURE WOULD BE NICE IF SOMEONE THREW ME A PARTY.

YEAH, BUT WHO?

IT WOULD HAVE TO BE SOMEONE WHO WOULD KNOW EXACTLY WHAT KIND OF PARTY I WOULD WANT WITHOUT EVEN ASKING ME!

WOW! LIKE ONE OF THOSE PSYCHIC MIND READERS!

I WAS THINKING OF SOMEONE LIKE YOU.

EXACTLY.

HA! THERE'S NO ONE LIKE ME!

I GOT IT! I'LL THROW YOU A PARTY!

GREAT IDEA! HOW DO YOU DO IT?

I JUST DO!

Johnny asked everyone
in class to come.

WILL YOU COME TO MY PARTY?

WELL...

I DIDN'T GET THAT.

WHAT DAY?

NICE SHIRT.

A PARTY, YOU SAY?

I FEEL A COLD COMING ON.

I HAVE A DENTIST APPOINTMENT.

YOU HAVE TO SPEAK INTO MY GOOD EAR.

OH BOY!

Everyone loved Gloria Crust, so naturally they all said they would come.

IT'S FOR GLORIA CRUST!

I'LL BE THERE!

COUNT ME IN!

SHOULD I BAKE A CAKE?

HOT DOG!

A PARTY, YOU SAY!

I FEEL BETTER SUDDENLY!

HOLD ON. MY MISTAKE. I'M FREE THAT DAY!

I HEAR YA, MISTER!

SHE'S MY GIRL!

Mutton was overflowing with ideas
for the party all week long.
The other kids were not impressed.

Mutton was so excited, he got up at five in the morning on Saturday and began waiting for his guests to arrive.

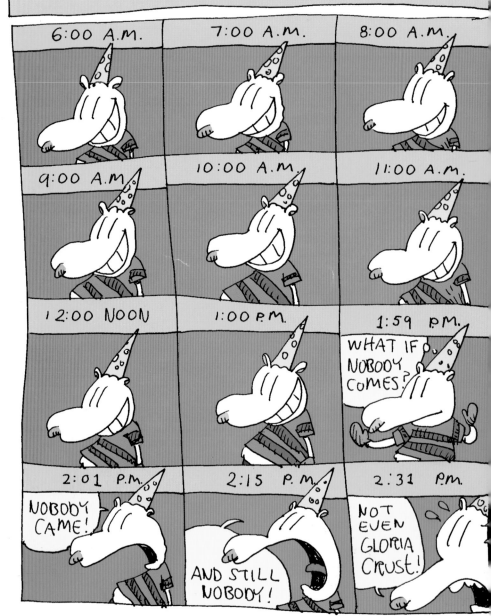

Just then Crust showed up. (She was always late.)

Johnny watched her eyes scan the empty room.

To this day, a better birthday party
has never been thrown.

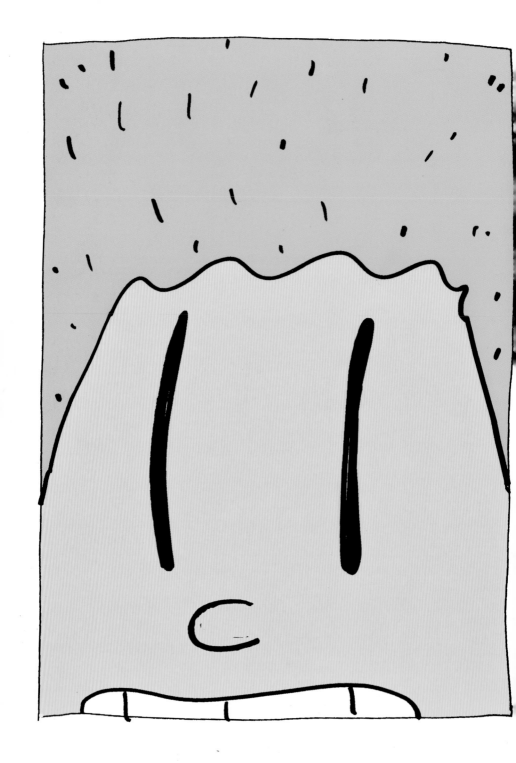

Driving Mrs. Torpolli Crazy

25

One day Johnny decided he would make Mrs. Torpolli love him. He went to her store and told her so.

TODAY I WILL MAKE YOU LOVE ME.

SHEESH.

YOU WANT ME TO LOVE YOU? HMMM. PUTTING MR. STOCKMAN'S GROCERIES IN A BAG WOULDN'T HURT YOUR CHANCES.

I'M ON IT, SISTA!

Mutton bagged all that day.
He was awful at it.

LEARN FROM JOHNNY'S MISTAKES.

MR. STOCKMAN'S BAG
DON'T THROW EGGS IN ONE AT A TIME.

LORETTA SMATZ'S BAG
NEVER BREAK BREAD INTO TINY PIECES SO IT WON'T STICK OUT OF THE BAG.

RICO ZANZABAR'S BAG
NO NEED TO TEST THE MILK BEFORE PACKING IT.

VIVIAN BLANKHEAD'S BAG
IT'S SILLY TO POUR KETCHUP INTO THE BAG SO THE LADY WON'T HAVE TO CARRY A HEAVY BOTTLE.

GET OUT AND STAY OUT!

Mrs. Torpolli told Johnny never to enter her store again. She was very angry.

But all that night customers called
Mrs. Torpolli on the phone.

THAT KID BAGGING THE GROCERIES WAS WONDERFUL!

MR. STOCKMAN

HE TOUCHED MY HEART.

LORETTA SMATZ

HE MADE MY DAY!

RICO ZANZABAR

I LOVE HIM! I JUST LOVE HIM!

VIVIAN BLANKHEAD

Apparently Mutton had written a poem on the back of each bag.

One dozen
eggs.
Six boxes
of Jell-O.
I like you.
I just had
to tello!

MR. STOCKMAN'S BAG

Stick O'
butter.
Loaf O'
bread.
I like you.
That's what
I said!

LORETTA SMATZ'S BAG

Steak and
potatoes.
Aluminum
foil.
I like you.
Don't let
the milk
spoil!

RICO ZANZABAR'S BAG

Ketchup from
a bottle.
Something in
a can.
I like you.
You da man!
(Even though
you're a lady.)

VIVIAN BLANKHEAD'S
BAG

The next day on her walk to work, Mrs. Torpolli figured out that Johnny had written all those poems for her.

When she got to work,
Mrs. Torpolli found one last poem.

Just then she spotted
Mutton, who thought she
was still angry with him.

Johnny never ran faster in his life.

The Staring Contest

34

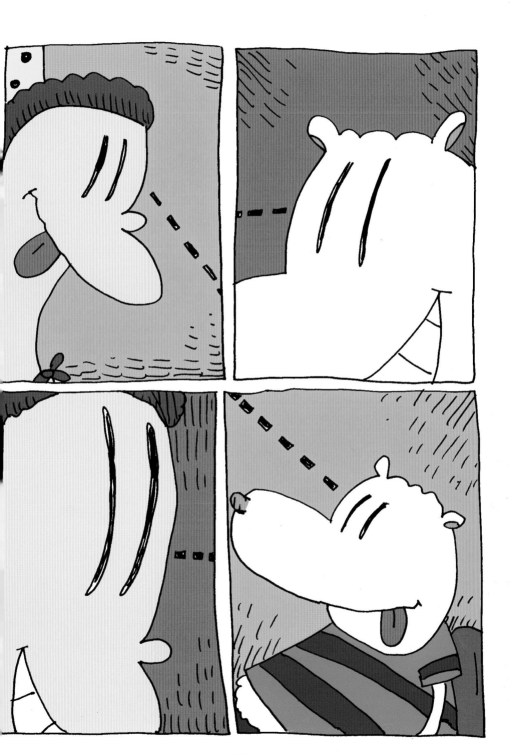

35

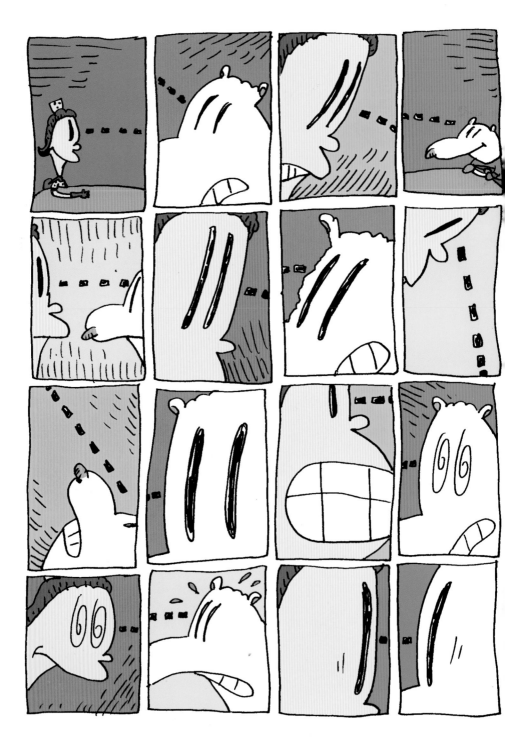

Johnny went on to become President of the World and brought about world peace by instituting "Give-an-Enemy-a-Cupcake Day."

On Gloria's next birthday, Johnny decided to outdo himself and throw her a party that even *he* wasn't invited to.

Rico Zanzabar, completely inspired by Johnny's poems, asked Loretta Smatz to marry him.

Rico Zanzabar's broken heart soon mended, and he asked Vivian Blankhead for *her* hand in marriage...with much better results.

Momma won the title
"Staring Champion of the Quad-State Area"
by deploying her secret weapon at just
the right moment.